THERAPY THOUGHTS
& Treats

ADALINE WINTERS

To Sophie,

Copyright © 2022 by Adaline Winters

All rights reserved

No part of this book may be reproduced, stored in a retrieval system, or transmitted by any means, electronic, mechanical, photocopying, recording or otherwise without the express written permission from the author.

Hope you enjoy!
Adaline Winters

"Writing is like a 'lust,' or like 'scratching when you itch.' Writing comes as a result of a very strong impulse, and when it does come, I, for one, must get it out."

C.S. Lewis

These characters have long lived rent free in my mind. I am not in control, they are. They have their own thoughts, feelings, desires and personalities. Occasionally a scene which doesn't' belong in their books pops into my head – and they won't be quiet until they are heard.

This book is the up to date accumulation of these scenes, messages, therapy sessions and more.

They can be enjoyed without you reading my books, but to understand their motivations and personalities – it is best to have read the books first.

They make me smile, and I'm hoping they will do that for you also.

For everyone who has taken a chance on me. Thank you for your encouragement, support and faith. I am forever grateful for each and everyone of you. All of you make this journey possible.

To my warriors and PA's who I often kidnap for inspiration, and find yourself thrown into therapy or scenes, without you these wouldn't exist.

THERAPY

The characters of The Hope Legacy and Cora Roberts have issues. They attend weekly meetings with Adaline to thrash out what's on their minds and hopefully lead them to fruitful relationships... or at the very least, less violent ones.

Session 1

I feel...

Adaline - Let's welcome our new members to the group, Cora And Hudson.

Cora - Don't say that like we're together.

Adaline - I would never presume.

Hudson - Of course not, the little witch thinks she's above me.

Natia - Dude, if she says you're not together, then you're not together. It takes two to tango.

Archan - If the man wants to claim her, don't get in the way. Shifters are possessive.

Natia - Are you freakin' kidding me?

Adaline - This is about expressing how we feel, use I statements rather than attacking another member of the group.

Hudson - I feel like claiming Cora.

Adaline - That's not what I mean.

Cora - and I feel like you are stuck in fantasy land.

Natia - I feel like the males in this room don't listen.

Adaline -

Archan - I feel that you need to listen to me.

Adaline - That's good Archan, you don't feel like Natia listens to you?

Natia - He's in my head, woman! Do you know how that feels?

Adaline - Actually, yes.

Cora - Hudson needs to back off and go back to the pack. He's trespassing on my land and my emotions.

Hudson - Cora needs to own up to her own emotions and admit she wants me.

Adaline - Sit down, Hudson. Can we come back to the I statements?

Archan - We got past that with Natia, her problem is running into danger and not sharing her idiotic plans.

Adaline - No? Okay.

Natia - Because you'd stop me.

Adaline -

Cora - They think we owe them every single facet of our lives.

Natia - Right? Yet they won't even tell us what they are!

Cora - I know what he is.

Natia - What?

Cora - Impossible.

Natia - 😂

Hudson - I'm not staying for this.

Archan - Agreed. <disappears>

Hudson - Well, fuck me. What is he?

Natia - I'm still figuring it out.

Adaline - 😏

Session 2

The Stick

Adaline - Welcome everyone, let's get started. For homework I asked you to bring a song which would depict how you feel about your relationship, and for clarity I have a talking stick, only the person holding the stick can talk. <Hands stick to Cora>

Cora - Wait, what? We have to share with the group?

Adaline - That's the point of group therapy.

Archan - Is it too late to change mine?

Natia - Why? Your feelings for me not good enough to be on show for the group? 😒

Archan - No, but I'm a private man.

Natia - fine, I'll change mine.

Archan - 🙂 Okay fine, we stay the course.

Adaline - Great, now that's settled. Cora?

Cora - (🎵🎵Never gonna get it, never gonna get it🎵🎵)

Cora - In case you missed the point, I'm telling you that you ain't ever getting me.

Hudson - We will see.

Cora - You'll see nothing.

Hudson - Next time we roll around half naked on your bedroom floor with our tongues warring, I'll remind you of this.

Natia - When was this?

Archan - Stay out of it woman. I've told you, shifters bite, they are only one step above Neanderthals.

Cora - Word.

Hudson - I have more self-control than that.

Natia - Archan, it's you who bites!

Adaline - Biting is not appropriate, we aren't two year olds. Also, use the talking stick.

Archan - <snaps fingers - talking stick appears in his hand> The bite represents a claim.

Hudson - Now who's a Neanderthal?

Adaline - Let's all calm down. Archan, would you like to share your song whilst you are holding the stick?

Archan - (🎵ain't no sunshine when she's gone...🎵)

Natia - 😳

Cora - 😘

Hudson - 😐 Get. A. Room.

Adaline - That's very insightful, you sound lost without Natia.

Archan - <throws stick at Natia>

Natia - I erm...

Adaline - Time for you to share, Natia.

Natia - 😬

Archan - What's wrong? Cat got your tongue? I can help with that.

Natia - 😐 (♪♪Love me like you do♪♪)

Archan - So you submit to me?

Natia - 😳 How'd you get that from a love song?

Archan - It's from a movie about submitting.

Adaline - Don't forget to use the stick.

Natia - You've watched Fifty Shades? 😂

Cora - Wow, what have you let yourself in for? Perhaps you should have asked for one of those contracts? Hard limits and all that.

Adaline - Stick? Anybody?

Archan - It's my job to push her limits.

Adaline - That's a no to the stick then?

Natia - I already know his tastes are on the kinky side.

Archan - Her shoulder isn't the only place I've bitten.

Natia - 😳

Hudson - Too much information. Plus finding out what makes your partner tick in the bedroom is half the fun.

Cora - Unless she's into fur and fangs, I'd say you're shit out of luck.

Hudson - You weren't complaining.

Adaline - Okayyyy... let's bring this back to topic. Natia, it sounds like a declaration of being open and vulnerable for the man you love?

Natia - Sure, let's go with that.

Adaline - You don't agree?

Natia - Adaline, this is your head. If you say I'm open and vulnerable to Archan, then I must be.

Adaline - Great-

Natia - But just so we are clear, I'm not vulnerable. I can be strong and open at the same time.

Adaline - Okay. Got it.

Natia - I mean, you don't have to be vulnerable to be in love, right?

Adaline - 👀

Cora - I think maybe, yes?

Archan - I agree with Natia, you don't need to be vulnerable to be in love.

Hudson - Sure, you do. How can you be 100% in love and not be vulnerable? You are giving the other person the power to crush your soul.

Archan - ......

Natia - ......

Adaline - Annndddd finally, Hudson could you share your song please?

Hudson - (🎶 See beneath your beautiful 🎶)

Cora - 😲

Natia - 🥰

Archan - 🥶

Session 3

Bad Life Choices

Adaline - You're all late. The session started 30 minutes ago.

Cora - Sorry, Adaline, we got held up.

Adaline - Doing what?

Natia - <goes to sit and misses, landing on the floor> Shopping?

Adaline - When you answer like it's a question, I know you are lying.

Natia - I can't lie.

Adaline - What did you shop for?

Archan and Hudson stumble into the room, bumping into each other whilst laughing.

Adaline - Are you drunk?

Archan - Don't be silly, woman, I don't get drunk.

Hudson - We're drunk.

Adaline - This is pointless. We can reschedule for tomorrow.

Cora <pulls bucket of popcorn from bag, opens it and offers Natia some>

Hudson - Where's my yummy treat?

Cora - 😒 Your yummy treat is probably waiting for you in your bed - the one back at the pack!

Natia - Oooh he's still driving you nuts on your land?

Cora - He prowls the grounds at crazy assed times of the night. He quizzes the delivery people like he's from the FBI. He's suspicious, possessive and an asshole.

Hudson - I do not act like I'm from the FBI.

Cora - What about that Tom?

Hudson - 😬

Natia - What happened with Tom?

<Door bangs open and in strolls Lucifer>

Natia - Lulu!

Lucifer - Good evening, everyone, let's get this party started.

Adaline - What are you doing here?

Lucifer - I'm here to ensure they behave, they've been drinking in my club.

Adaline - <glares at the gang> Seriously?

Natia - Snitches get stitches.

Lucifer - Temptress, the only one getting stitches will be you as you fall on your own ass aided by nothing but your inability to take your alcohol like a real man.

Natia - I'm not a real man, I'm all woman.

Lucifer - Noted. You've been naked enough for me to know you have dimples on the bottom of your back.

Archan - What? He's seen you naked?

Lucifer - Who hasn't?

Cora - Me.

Hudson - Because we exist in separate worlds.

Cora - But we are here now. No reason she can't be naked in whatever wacked out place we are in.

Adaline - That would be my head.

Natia - Are you suggesting I get naked?

Archan - Absolutely not.

Cora - Yes.

Lucifer - <leans back and crosses his ankles - evil smirk firmly in place> My work here is done.

Natia - That would just be weird to take my clothes off.

Archan - Natia prefers to be naked by circumstance, not by her own free will.

Cora - I'll get naked with you if it makes you feel better.

Adaline - 🙍

Hudson - Pass the popcorn.

Cora - No, it's mine.

Hudson - Where are you going to stash it, little witch? You're about to get naked in order to see another woman naked.

Adaline - No nakedness.

Hudson - Wait, is that why you won't be with me? You like women?

Cora - 🙂 Because the only possible reason I'm not rolling on my back and spreading my legs for you is because I prefer women?

Hudson - I don't have a preference for you being on your back.

Cora - That's not what I meant.

Hudson - Against the wall, on your knees—hell, you can be on top if you prefer.

Cora - There's a special word for you.

Hudson - Ooh what? Alpha? Delicious? Sexy?

Cora - Conceited.

Natia - He's sexy too though.

Cora - Yes, but he knows it.

Natia - Yeah, I have one of those. <jumps up and starts dancing whilst breaking out into "I'm too sexy for my shirt" and shimmying it off over her shoulders>

Archan - 🙂 This is how she ends up naked.

Session 4

Why Have Enemies When You Can Have Friends Like These?

Adaline - Welcome newcomers, you're each here as an advocate for your friend. Let's get introductions done. Natia, you go first.

Natia - This is Duncan, my best friend and he's a warlock.

Cora - Warlock? Is that like a witch?

Duncan - No.

Natia - Touchy subject.

Adaline - Now you, Cora.

Cora - This is Sebastian, my oldest friend, he's a vampire prince.

Natia - You drink blood?

Sebastian- Yes.

Natia - You drink her blood?

Hudson - Touchy subject.

Adaline - Now you, Hudson.

Hudson - This is Dave, chief of security.

Archan - You expecting a fight?

Dave - No, but you can never be too careful. If these two want to hash it out, that's mate business.

Cora - There is no mate business, because there is no mate.

Adaline - And finally, Archan.

Archan - This is Zac, head of security.

Hudson - Huh.

Archan - what?

Hudson - We both brought protection against the women we want. Not sure what that says about us.

Zac - That you can't be trusted to think with your brains rather than your balls.

Dave - That's right, we are the brains.

Cora - Not the B word I would associate with you.

Dave - And what B word would you use, undertaker?

Cora - Bread.

Natia - Ohh bread ☺

Duncan - Undertaker?

Cora - An unfortunate nickname some buffoon came up with. That's it!

Hudson - What's it?

Cora - Buffoon, that's your B word, Dave.

Natia - Good one. My nickname is Locks.

Adaline - If we can just get back to why we are here?

Archan - I don't have a nickname.

Zac - Me either, we are gods, above nicknames.

Natia - 😳

Archan - 😳

Zac - What? I don't have a nickname.

Everyone - ....

Zac - 😶

Adaline - Zac, take your seat please. There's no nickname.

Natia - It's not bad.

Adaline - 🙍

Archan - It's nothing to do with me.

Zac - JUST SPIT IT OUT.

Natia - It's informative.

Zac - I swear to the creator, woman... if you do not-

Natia - Paddy Waddy Zaccy.

Zac - 😶

Cora - 🤣

Zac - I do not have paddies.

Adaline - Right, moving on. The idea here is that your advocates can see things about you that you may not recognize. Perhaps give you an insight into your relationship issues.

Natia - So, they are doing your job?

Adaline - What? No.

Natia - But you're the pseudo therapist who's having group meetings with fictional characters in your head.

Cora - Yeah, maybe you should be in therapy.

Duncan - Stop picking on Adaline.

Adaline - Thank you, Duncan.

Sebastian - You know you just thanked yourself, right?

Adaline - Would you like to survive book 2?

Natia - 😬

Archan - I know you are newish to Adaline's world, but she's a ruthless monster with no hang ups on sacrificing a main character.

Hudson - How main?

Natia - 😬

Adaline - If it's necessary for the plot, I won't hesitate.

Hudson - And what do you think that says about you?

Adaline - Nothing.

Dave - 😟

Adaline - What?

Zac - I think it says you are a psycho taking out your issues on unsuspecting characters in your books.

Adaline - Again, do you want to survive book 3?

Zac - At this point I'd be surprised if anyone survives.

Adaline - 😶

Cora - Maybe you should bring a friend next time, Adaline?

Adaline - Errr no.

Zac - Why, because you have none?

Adaline - Do you know what the delete key does on a keyboard?

Natia - Gets rid of bad decisions?

Hudson - Yeah, and replace them with worse ones.

Sebastian - Speaking of bad decisions, I heard a rumour about Dave and Adaline.

Adaline - Sebastian, back away from the gossip.

Dave - 😏

Cora - Ohhh what?

Natia - Yeah, spill the beans.

Archan - Anything that can be used as blackmail to return Natia to me will be greatly rewarded.

Adaline - Sebastian...

Cora - Rewarded like how?

Archan - You want Hudson off your property?

Cora - Yup.

Hudson - Liar.

Archan - Consider it done.

Hudson - Try it, buddy, and those pretty feathers of yours will be lining my pillow tonight.

Sebastian - So Dave is apparently based off Adaline's actual husband.

Cora - 😱

Hudson - 🤔

Natia - 😟

Archan - 😶

Duncan - 😐

Adaline - Duncan, what's wrong?

Duncan - Nothing.

Natia - Dude, you can't huff and not tell her.

Adaline - Tell me what?

Duncan - I thought I was your fictional husband.

Adaline - Oh erm 😬

Dave - Nope, that's me. 😏

Hudson - Your husband grows fur and howls at the moon?

Adaline - 🙍

David - Only on weekends.

Therapy Session 5

The Line

Hudson - Why he is here?

Cora - Where's Adaline?

Lucifer - On vacation.

Natia - Ohh anywhere nice?

Lucifer - I have no idea. Some Scottish hideaway.

Cora - Aww how romantic.

Hudson - I can take you a Scottish castle.

Cora - Nooo thank you. Please feel free to pack your suitcase and move there, on your own.

Archan - So we get to skip therapy this week?

Lucifer - Absolutely not. We are doing therapy the devil style.

Natia - 🗿

Cora - What's the devil style?

Lucifer - Tell me your darkest desires.

Cora - Did he just reference from The Lucifer show?

Lucifer - Nonsense, he stole it from me.

Cora - Wow, that's quite the ego.

Natia - Yes, well that's the thing-

Hudson - Dude, you've let that name go to your head; every second baby is called Lucifer now.

Natia - That would be all the males then?

Cora - That's where you stole that line from, admit it. You are a wannabe Lucifer.

Lucifer - <Rises to his feet. Unbuttons his suit jacket, drops it to the floor, followed by his shirt>.

Archan - Brother, there's no need for theatrics.

Cora - Is this naked thing a problem with all of you guys in the Hope Legacy?

Lucifer - <pure white wings explode from his back lifting him off the ground>.

Cora - Fuck me.

Hudson - Holy Shit.

Natia - That's what I was trying to tell you.

Cora - You're the devil.

Lucifer - The one and only.

Hudson - I need a drink.

Lucifer - Afterwards. We will first discuss your darkest desires.

Cora - 😂😂😂😂

Lucifer - What's funny?

Cora - I just... you can't just say that line and keep a straight face. You're the devil.

Lucifer - Exactly.

Cora - 😂😂😂😂

Natia - 😂😂😂😂 can't breathe 😂😂😂😂

Lucifer - at this point I'm not sure I want to know the darkest desires of you two. You're nuts. There's no helping you, I'll tell Adaline my conclusion.

Cora - You will do no such thing. It's the only thing keeping me sane whilst Adaline dawdles writing the final Hope book.

Natia - Pinky promise, Lulu, I need this session with my girl Cora. 🥺

Lucifer - Fine, she's back next week anyway. She can deal with your crazy asses.

Hudson - What exactly was this session about?

Lucifer - Telling me your darkest desires.

Hudson - <snaps fingers at Archan> Pay up.

Archan - He said it twice.

Cora - Nope definitely three times.

Natia - Pay the man, Archan, you lost the bet.

Lucifer - Bet?

Natia - Sorry, Lulu, we bet Hudson couldn't get you to say that line three times.

Lucifer - What line?

Natia - Are you being serious?

Lucifer - What line? 😊

Natia - Tell me your darkest desires.

Lucifer - <snaps fingers at Archan>. Pay up, brother, I got her to say it.

Natia - 😊

Therapy Session 6

Introducing...

Adaline - Let's talk about sex.

Zee - Baby.

Natia - Let's talk about you and.

Zee - Me.

Adaline - no no no.

Zee - Let's talk about all the good things and the bad-

Adaline - Stop. For the love of… <looks at Archan> just stop.

Cora - Who invited the freaky guy?

Zee - Have we met?

Adaline - The session is about sex, I couldn't keep him out.

Zee - I am the expert.

Natia - How? Of all the people here you've got the least amount of action.

Hudson - Even I got a fumble and a kiss.

Archan - Myself and Natia beat you all.

Cora - Yeah yeah big guy you got the big kahonas.

Adaline - If we can just focus for a second.

Hudson - If you'd care to inspect I'm sure I would measure up.

Natia - I can grab a ruler if you like?

Adaline - No rulers.

Zee - I am but a mortal, but I outman you guys. Get the ruler.

Adaline - This is meant to be a safe space to explore your sexual experiences and discuss if there is more you need from partner.

Hudson - I actually just need it to begin with.

Natia - <disappears and reappears a few seconds later brandishing a six inch ruler.>

Archan - Woman, I make you scream. Don't wave that tiny stick at me.

Hudson - Right, is that for the freak over there. <Points at Zee>

Adaline - We need to get back on topic.

Zee - When you are ready to learn how to satisfy a woman, call me. 😉

Adaline - <Jumps up and points at Archan> You need to learn to not use sex to distract Natia and yourself from the bigger issues.

Archan - 😳 What bigger issues?

Adaline - The apocalypse. <Points at Natia> And you, young lady, need to stop letting him. Take control. Tie him down and have your wicked way, it's empowering and he'll secretly enjoy it.

Natia - Technically I'm way way older than you, Adaline.

Adaline - You sure about that?

Natia - 😱

Adaline - <Points at Hudson> Stop trying to get in her panties and actual listen to Cora. Feel her heart, her soul, her love. When you stop trying to have sex, you'll get it.

Hudson - Are you saying I have a one track mind?

Cora - You moved onto my property. That's class A stalker behavior.

Hudson - I did it to plug a weak spot on your property.

Cora - And I suppose you take midnight strolls outside my bedroom window for 'security reasons'.

Hudson - I was patrolling the grounds. You were infiltrated by your own kind trying to murder you.

Cora - Then keep your eyes on the grounds and off my window as I prepare for bed.

Hudson - You could just shut the curtains.

Zee - Tease.

Adaline - Cora, it's about time you let someone in. Stop clinging to the notion all men will hurt you.

Natia -

Cora - Fine, singles night at the house is in a few weeks. I'll find a man.

Hudson - I'll be there.

Cora - You're not invited.

Zee - What's your address, beautiful?

Adaline - And, Zee….

Zee - Yes, Adaline?

Adaline - Everybody enjoys a flirt, but you need to find that special lady you want to dedicate all your flirting power to.

Zee - I don't understand? You are suggesting I tie myself down?

Adaline - Yes.

Zee - No.

Adaline - Why not? I can write you a lovely woman.

Zee - Because all this <gestures down body> is too much for one woman. I want a harem.

Lily - dude, that's my jam. Women aren't interested in reading about one guy with lots of women. 😐

Zee - Who the fu*k are you?

Natia - I thought she was like the refreshments chick or something?

Archan - Trust your mind to attribute the presence of a stranger to food delivery.

Cora - So who the hell are you?

Lily - 😉

Therapy Session 7

While the author is away you know damn straight the PAs are here to play.

Natia - why do you have talking stick?

Archan - Adaline asked me to bring it back.

Zac - Because it worked so well last time. 😐

Natia - Why are you wearing a bow tie?

Duncan - On the group chat it said to wear a bow.

Door opens and two women waltz in.

Liberty - The message said wear only a bow.

Zoe - That's right, we left the color choice to you.

Liberty - (sighs) Simple instructions gang.

Door opens - Zee struts in.

Natia - OMG my eyes I can't unsee it.

Zee - What? The message said wear only a bow.

Door opens - Jed strides in.

Zee - He got the memo!

Archan - You're idiots.

Zoe - Naked idiots, they are forgiven, take a seat boys. We are just waiting for the rest of the Therapy gang.

Natia - They can't sit on these seats like that! Their bits will touch them.

Archan - I love that you are a freak with me and a prude to the world.

Door opens - Cora and Hudson walk in.

Cora - Sorry we are late, Hudson had a furry moment.

Hudson - He smelled like catnip. Not my fault.

Cora - Why are you guys naked?

Jed - We're not. We are wearing bows.

Cora - Alrighty then.

Hudson - Who the hell are you two?

Liberty - We are the PA's.

Natia -

Cora - Oh shit, what did you guys do? Adaline has brought in the big guns.

Zoe - What do you think they did?

Jed - Say nothing, they know nothing, don't incriminate yourself.

Zee - 😬

Jed - No, Zee, there's no evidence.

Liberty - 🤔 Evidence of what.

Zee - He deserved it.

Jed - Dude!

Zee - I can't help it. She's got that stare…

Hudson - Wait, where's Adaline?

Zoe - In her writing cave.

Hudson - Oh that old chestnut. 🙄

Liberty - Do you want another book?

Hudson - 🤐

Archan - Why do I have this stick?

Liberty - Oooo that's for me. Can you make it appear in my hand?

Stick appears in liberty's hand.

Liberty - 🥰

Natia - What are you going to do with the stick.

Liberty tucks it away in her handbag.

Liberty - 😳 Me? Nothing!

Natia - Is this a sanctioned therapy session?

Cora - Yeah, does Adaline know you've invaded her head?

Zoe - Of course!

Liberty - But times up, thanks for the stick!

Zoe and Liberty run out of room.

Duncan - I'm not convinced that stick is going to be used for therapeutic purposes.

Therapy session 8

New Girl

Adaline - Good evening everyone. It's been awhile since our last session.

Zee - you abandoned us.

Adaline - I did not. I was working on something.

Lucifer - My book?

Adaline - 😬

Duncan - It's mine, I'm her favorite.

Adaline - Um…

Cora - Wait your turn boys. I'm unfinished.

Hudson - Yesh, I definitely have blue-

Adaline - Okay, okay, I'm working on Cora's new book. Plus something else.

Archan - (Appears out of thin air with his wings sweeping out).

Natia - Quite the entrance.

Archan - I was picking up the new girl. (Pulls out a wide eyed woman from behind him).

Natia - Who the hell is that?

Archan - Calm down, wife. This is Rie. She's from the group.

Cora - Oooo a fan?

Natia - 🙂 Like you need any more ego boost.

Adaline - actually I asked him to bring her.

Rie - (waves) Hi.

Zee - New girl? Ooo, how you doin?

Adaline - Did you seriously just steel a line from Joey?

Natia - Rie, come sit here between me and Cora, otherwise you'll suffocate with BDE.

Adaline - BDE?

Natia - Big d*ck energy.

Adaline - 😳

Cora - Yeah we can protect you. Sit down, come tell us about yourself.

Rie - Takes a seat between the girls. Um, I'm not sure why Archan just kidnapped me from my family dinner.

Natia - What were you having?

Rie - Meatballs.

Natia - Next time we meet at Rie's. The snacks in Adaline's head suck.

Cora - Still doesn't explain why she's here.

Archan - Adaline told me too.

Adaline - I said - go speak to her, and give her an update on where my head is at with writing.

Archan - Mission accomplished. She's in your head. You can't get any more updated than that.

Duncan - Tell us about yourself, Rie.

Rie - Okay. My favorite color is black.

Lucifer - A girl after my heart.

Zee - You don't have a heart.

Lucifer - Wrong, I'm missing a soul. But that's another story. (Eyeballs Adaline) for Adaline to get her finger out her ass and write.

Rie - I also love red.

Natia - Now you're talking.

Zee - Where exactly do you like red?

Rie - 😳

Duncan - Stop it, Zee. No underwear discussion in therapy.

Adaline - That's right, we made that a rule. Tell us more, Rie.

Rie - I love reading. Pride and prejudice is a favorite.

Zee - Like role play? Women in that era wore corsets and pantaloons.

Adaline -

Rie - I also love the movie Date with an Angel.

Lucifer - Really. Do tell me more.

Zee - You're the devil.

Lucifer - (Stands up).

Cora - Oh no, he's going to do the whole wing reveal thing again.

Lucifer - (Wings snap out and span meters). I'm the archangel Lucifer. God's favorite child.

Archan - Were. You were God's favorite.

Lucifer - I helped save the world.

Rie - (reaches out to touch the wing.)

Natia - Unless you're ready to get your freak on with the devil, I suggest you don't do that.

Adaline - Put your wings away, Lucifer. New rule - no wings in therapy.

Cora - I'll add it to the list.

Rie - I have two children.

Zee - Married? Please say no.

Natia - bloody hell, I'm surrounded by one track minded idiots.

Rie - Yes, I'm married.

Zee - Damn.

Adaline - Stop it.

Zee - Who me? I'm just being nice. Do you plan on him being forever, or are you looking for your next one?

Rie - Forever.

Hudson - Ignore him. What do you do for a living?

Rie - I'm a manager.

Zee - Dominating? I can get on board with that.

Duncan - Married, Zee. Leave her alone.

Zee - Sorry, Rie. (Pouts and bats his eyelashes).

Rie - I'm also a writer.

Natia - Oooo another imaginative mind to play!

Cora - That's so cool. You can come back.

Adaline - Am I being replaced?

Natia - Take a holiday.

Cora - Go write my book. Rie has got this.

Rie - Um, it's okay thanks. I have enough on my plate.

Duncan - 🤐 Rejection hurts.

Hudson - It's fine, Adaline created us. And like kids, she's responsible for us. Right?

Everyone - (looks around the room).

Zee - She left.

Archan - You told her to take a holiday, I suspect she's halfway to beach by now.

Natia - Damn it. Rie, you stay. We can't be left unsupervised.

Everyone - (looks around the room).

Lucifer - She also left.

Natia - Damn it again. I wanted meatballs.

Zee - Always with the food, woman.

Archan - We are unsupervised… let the games begin.

MESSAGES

Text messages hold an intriguing insight into my characters lives. Enjoy!

The Fridge

Natia - So you know that unidentified body?

Zee - Which one?

Natia - There's more than one?

Zee - Check the fridge.

Natia - .... I can only see the fresh one.

Zee - Not the body fridge, the food fridge.

Duncan - Please tell me you didn't put it in there.

Aaden - What did you do?

Zee - Wait for it.

Natia - WTF!

Zee - One, nil.

Natia - You put severed leprechaun parts in with my lasagna leftovers!! You're evil, pure evil.

Duncan - I'll pick something up on my way over.

Duncan - Chinese or Italian?

Duncan - Natia?

Natia - Don't bother, I've picked out the bits and It's making its merry way around the microwave now.

Aaden - That's unsanitary.

Zee - She eats any meat.

Aaden - Not true, she doesn't like lamb.

Zee - That's not what I meant.... I was referring to (delete) you're right, she doesn't.

Aaden - Natia, are you talking about the demon with the horn?

Natia - Yes the unihorn.

Duncan - That's not a thing.

Natia - It is now.

Jed - You're eating leprechaun leftovers?

Natia - How did you get on the group chat?

Zee - I invited him.

Aaden - You didn't clear that with me.

Jed - Don't be mad, you can't have the Scooby gang without shaggy.

Natia - Buffy needs her Zander.

Zee - I thought I was Zander?

Natia - Nope, you're Spike.

Duncan - Here she goes.

Zee - Buffy and Spike end up together don't they?

Natia - Eventually, but he's a rebound from Angel.

Zee - I'll take it. Who's Giles?

Natia - Hang on...

Jed - Where'd she go?

Duncan - Natia, what's wrong with the body?

Aaden - I'm in the Rec room. I'll go find her.

Jed - Duncan, you are so Giles.

Duncan - I have no idea what you're talking about.

Zee - Are you picking up food for the rest of us, or does princess Waterford get special treatment?

Duncan - The leprechaun wasn't poisoned was it?

Natia - Stop stressing! I was going to ask why his heart was still beating.

Zee - Why was it still beating?

Natia - I don't know.

Aaden - She cut it out.

Zee - What?

Natia - It's fine I stored it with your beers.

The Bodyguard

Archan - Your bodyguard is staring at me in a murderous manner. You need to get your delectable ass back to this meeting before I remove his eyes.

Natia - Who? Zee.

Archan - The tall one with short hair and green eyes.

Natia - Don't be making eyes at my bodyguard. He might get the wrong idea, and he's a freak in bed.

Archan - You and him? When.

Natia - That's not what I meant.

Archan - He will die a long and painful death.

Natia - Ugh, put your penis back in your pants. I'm sure yours is bigger.

Archan - And how would you know that?

Natia - I don't! It's a guess because right now you are being the bigger dick.

Natia - Stop staring at Archan he's getting the wrong idea.

zee - He's a dick

Natia -

Out

Archan - Where are you?

Natia - Out.

Archan - Could you be more specific?

Natia - Yes.

Archan - Tell me where you are.

Natia - Out.

Jed - I'm with her, she's safe.

Natia - That's debatable.

Zee - Why do you want to know?

Archan - I need to speak with you.

Natia - Why you want to discuss how much your obsession with me crosses the border in stalker territory?

Archan - If you are not careful I will take you over my knee and show you how far across the line I can go.

Jed - Way to bring it home bro.

Zee - This fits the kinky side of you doesn't it Natia?

Archan - I'll show you a kinky side. (Delete). Just tell me where you are.

Archan - Natia?

Natia - Ohh big boy, come and show me just how kinky you can be. My bare skin is begging for your hand print.

Archan - Really? (Delete.) Then tell me where you are.

Natia - I don't think I could handle you.

Archan - What? I thought you'd be bringing me to my knees.

Natia - I'd be the one on my knees

Archan - Jed give Natia her phone back.

Jed - I can't she dancing.

Zee - With a guy.

Jed - Make it two.

Freak Panties

Natia - Okay who moved my freak panties off the bed?

Aaden - Moved what?

Zee - Freak panties?

Natia - Damn autocorrect. WHY THE HELL DOES MY PHONE KEEP CHANGING THE WORD FREAK TO FRESH? GRR YOU KNOW WHAT I MEAN.

Jed - No need to get your panties in a twist

Zee - She doesn't have any.

Natia - If I have to come out of this room naked to find my freak panties I will shove them down your throat.

Zee - I'm really not sure where the threat is in that message.

Natia - You're such a fresh.

Jed - A what?

Natia - You swapped the words fresh and freak in my phone somehow.

Aaden - Ah, that's why you wanted to know how to do it.

Archan - I have no understanding why you would messaging anyone about your fresh freak panties but me.

Natia - Fresh freak or freak fresh?

Jed - The first one sounds like it you change your panties all the time.

Zee - Whilst the second suggests you rarely change them - so if they are fresh it's freaky.

Natia - You are both fresh.

Archan - And you are pantiless, I will be there shortly.

THOUGHTS

Ever wondered what the White Furry Menace is really thinking? Or how Trevor and Natia's movie night's play out. What about speed dating Adaline style? Here is a collection of scenes that give extra insight into these characters.

Movie Night

Armed with salty popcorn and The exorcist, I sweep into Duncan's apartment. It was the first Saturday of the month, and that meant one thing - movie night with Trevor, my new bestie in Greed.

Trevor looked up from his sprawled position on the floor. "Pandora!" He shot to his feet and a squeal erupts from him as I wave the movie in his face. He does a little happy dance whilst dressed in a victor's outfit, complete with rosary beads.

"You. Look. Amazeballs," he gushes, taking my hand and spinning me around. My white nightgown had bits of oatmeal clinging to it, faking sick was difficult. But I'd managed a possessed look, with pale makeup and lank hair.

He grabs the DVD as I flop on the sofa. "Hey, Trevor, how was your month? That vampire bitch still giving you hell?"

He rolls his eyes. "If I'd known he was going to be a stage five clinger, I'd have forgone my night of passion."

"No, you wouldn't," I snort.

He glances over his shoulder as he shoves the dvd on the player. "No you're right, I wouldn't have. The sex was," he licks his fingers and swipes it in the air making a hissing noise.

The door bangs open and Jed and Zee stumble through the door. I slap my hand over my mouth. They are in matching black and red striped tops, hats, and one of their hands has plastic blades protruding from it, the other is armed with snacks. Jed's eyes go wide. "Dude, I thought we were doing Nightmare on Elm Street this month? It was in the group chat!"

Zee folds his arms and glares at me. "Definitely was in the group chat."

I arch a brow. "If you recall, we boycotted it when you decided I would be the half-naked damsel in distress."

Zee grabs his phone and swipes it before releasing a huff. "You need to get better reception."

"In Hell?" Trevor frowns. "Don't you have satanphone coverage?"

"Is that a thing?" I ask as the boys throw themselves onto the sofas.

Trevor rolls his eyes. "It's not like we have Virgin down here."

"Huh, I could have sworn he was a demon," I lamented.

The movie blasted onto the wide screen. "Hey, did you find out if Constantine was based on a real person?" Jed asks as he passes the Pringles over my head to Trevor.

"Apparently so."

"Wow," Zee mutters. "He's my hero."

My phone beeps. I slide it out of my nightgown pocket. "How come you get coverage?" Zee asks.

I frown. "It's Archan, maybe it's a god thing."

"We said no partners. You promised after the last time."

I glare at the phone.

Archan - Where did you put my keys?
Natia - On the hook next to the door - like always.
Archan - They aren't there.

Jed leans over my shoulder. "Lame excuse for harassing your wife, bro."

Natia - They totally are.

Archan - I need you to come home and check for me. I can only do "male searching?"

Natia - I'll send Lulu.

Archan - Also a male. It has to be you.

Natia - Then I'll send Emi.

Archan - I can come to you.

Natia - How would that help you find your keys?

Jed snatches the phone off me.

Natia - Bro, your girl is safe with us. Chill and go see Zac for a drink or something.

Archan - Jed? Why are you there? I thought this was a night with a demon.

I grab the phone back off him. "Awesome, now he will be relentless."

Archan - Natia, I will be joining you shortly.

Natia - No! Not after last time. I'm still mourning the loss of my clown suit.

Archan - You were covered in blood, I needed to see where you bleeding from.

Natia - Fake blood.

Archan - Same difference.

Natia - You caused me to be naked in front of my friend.

Archan - That appears to be a rite of passage for all your friends.

Natia - It's a new era.

Archan - Even our mail man has seen you naked.

Natia - One time! I forgot the towels in the dryer. So sue me if I refuse to put clothes on my wet body.

Jed snorts, so I glare at him.

Natia - I will be home in less than 3 hours. Sit tight and I'll see you in bed later . We can use the headboard…

Archan - You play dirty. Fine.

I throw the phone on the coffee table and swing my feet up before popping open the bag of popcorn and stuffing ten pieces in my mouth.

"He's not coming, right?" Trevor says glancing around the room like the god of darkness might just step out the shadows. I mean he can do that - but it's not his style.

"Nope, he tucked up in bed like a good little husband waiting for me."

"When is the human wedding?" Trevor asks. "Girl, you will look gorgeous in red. Please say you are kicking the norm and having a red dress."

I shrug. "Not decided yet on the date or the dress."

"It's a little redundant now he made you his super-duper soul mate," Zee mutters.

I throw popcorn at him. "The wedding is for everyone. It's a public claiming in my culture."

"Are exorcisms real?" Zee asks watching as the leading man visits the poor possessed girl.

Trevor tips his hand side to side. "Kind of. Not like this with a vicar and holy water. But the right words, with the right setup will see a demon banished. The host is normally already dead though."

"So the church doesn't have exorcists?"

Trevor side eyes me as he slurps on his cola. "They do. But they are less bible bearing and more demon bashing than this one." He points at the TV.

"How?"

He jumps up and grabs my hands pulling me to follow him. "Okay lay on the dining table," he motions to it. I hurry over, gather the hem of my nightgown and lay on my back. Jed and Zee turn to watch us over the back of the sofa.

"So the possessed just spits out curses and nasty words," Trevor says looking at me expectantly.

I roll my eyes.

"Oooo role play," Jed says.

I snort. Trevor folds his arms. "Fine. Your god can't save you father. Your sins have already damned your rotten soul to Hell. Grrr," I growl for effect. Zee and Jed snigger.

Trevor raises his hands and fire erupts in a circle around us.

"Ooo pretty," I breathe.

"Don't break character," he grinds out.

"Oh right. I am a wicked wicked demon who eats baby's hearts and paints the walls red with the blood of your parents."

"Is that the parents of the baby whose heart you ate?" Zee asks.

"Be gone you wicked whore. Go back to the depths of Hell that you dragged yourself from and leave this soul to eternal rest."

I jerk on the dining table, milking my part for all its worth.

"Be gone demon." Trevor shouts and lifts his cross at me.

The door bangs open and a huge form tears through the room. He throws Trevor into the wall and scoops me up.

"What have you done?" He roars his eyes swirling with a molten gold.

I tap his arm. "Hey, it's me."

He frowns. "What?"

"It's me we were just role playing the exorcist."

He jerks back. "There's something seriously wrong with you."

"My movie night, my rules."

He clenches his jaw, releases me and picks up a dazed Trevor. Who promptly swoons in Archan's arms and lays a hand on his own forehead. "My dark knight in Armani."

I huff as I swing my legs off the table. Archan snaps out his hand trying to catch me, I'm quicker as a goddess though, and instead he snags my nightgown and it tears clean off my body.

I glare down at myself. Jed and Zee fist pump behind Archan's back.

"Double feature movie night," Jed declares. "Now we have our damsel in distress."

"I'm no freaking damsel, Smoothie."

"That would be me," Trevor declares.

Archan spins Trevor upright and takes a step away from him. "God save me, I'm surrounded by crazy."

"You love my brand of crazy," I point out.

He smirks. "True, let's see how crazy we can get. You promised me bed action, woman." He slaps my ass before the world tilts and we arrive seconds later in our bedroom. He points at the bed.

"Naked, Natia, now."

A small smile dances on my lips. "Yes, husband."

Speed Dating

Summer grove house had been transformed into an oasis of romantic lighting and mood music. Ed Sheeran crooned about his beautiful woman. Lucky girl, any woman being serenaded by his dulcet tones was bound to fall at his feet.

Heels clacked up the steps as our next guest arrived. We'd had to make it an invite only list, turns out singles night *supernatural* style was a hit.

"Ah yes, Miss. Nolf, if you'd just follow this charming gentleman - he'll show you to your seat," I said, waving a hand at Sebastian who was offering Jennifer-Lynn his arm. Vampires could be counted on to be true gentlemen. At least until the biting… yikes, I hope Jennifer-Lynn was okay with what she'd let herself in for.

"Mrs," Jennifer-Lynn stated. She was a pretty woman who was rocking 1950's glam with pin curls and scarlet lipstick.

I cocked a brow and tapped my pen on the clipboard. "Excuse me?"

"I'm married."

Sebastian paused and darted a look between us. Seriously?

"This is a singles night, being married defeats the object," I huffed.

"I'm available for a fictional boyfriend."

"A what?"

"Fictional boyfriend, like where you fantasize about someone you read about."

I darted a look at Sebastian, was this chick nuts? "I see, and why would you consider coming to Sumemrgrove's singles evening for such a liaison?"

Jennifer-Lynn frowned. Then abruptly burst out laughing, almost doubling over. "Good one, Cora, like you don't know. Very good, I'll stay in character."

My eyes widened and Sebastian and I exchanged our 'crazy lady on the scene' look. You'd be surprised how often it happened, so much so, we had an actual look perfected. He ushered the laughing woman away just in time for my new friends to arrive.

"Natia! Thank you for coming, I know you are mated, but I appreciate the moral support."

The blond goddess, with legs that went on for days, spun in a circle so that her red floaty dress fanned out around her. "Wouldn't miss it for the world ending."

Archan, her tall, dark, and brooding mate swept up the stairs behind her, his giant wings snapped closed and she held out a shirt to him. "Put this on, before you cause a riot."

I glanced back in the house finding Mrs. Nolf's gaze on Archan's abs. Archan yanked his shirt on, dropped a kiss onto Natia's lips then swept into the house. Zee, Duncan, and Zac jogged up the steps behind them.

"Boys," I greeted with a wink.

Zee wolf whistled. "That dress looks amazing on you," he commented.

"Thank you, Zee."

He winked. "Of course it would look even better on my bedroom floor."

A growl rumbled around us in stereo, like we were surrounded by a pack of angry cats. I sighed, in reality it was one really big angry cat.

Zee glanced around trying to hunt the source of noise. The boys groaned and pushed him into the house before being intercepted by Maggie who was gathering up the men in the dining room. "If you'll follow me," she said. "Please hold your bad jokes and flirting for the main event."

"Nonsense, Maggie, I'm too good looking to save it until later. It's a constant stream of sexiness. I can't help it."

I rolled my eyes just as a heavy thud rocked the floorboards beneath my feet.

"You're not invited," I said to the big oaf.

Hudson waved a pink card hand decorated with silver glitter at me. "This says otherwise."

Damn it Maggie. As usual he was testing the workmanship of Henley and Levi's. So far they held up, more's the pity.

Wait, what? Ugh, this was going to be a long night.

"You can't come, then the number of males and females won't be balanced," I tried.

Dangerous Dave arrived in a sweep of leather and scowls. "You aren't invited either."

Dave cocked a brow at me. "We invited two extra women, the numbers work - ask Maggie."

I glanced over my shoulder and straight into the little bobcat shifter's eyes. She looked left and right, like there could be anyone else responsible for this, before scampering down the hallway into the kitchen. That's right, run for your life.

"Who are the females?" I asked turning back to Hudson and Dave. Nope wait, make that just Hudson. Dangerous Dave had somehow sneaked into my home, right under my nose.

"Jazzy and April."

"Sounds like members of a 90's band."

"Jealous?"

"No, I need their names for my list." I tapped my clipboard with my pen.

"Now you have them."

I rolled my eyes and stepped back to let the Terror of Tennessee into my home. He smelled so freakin' good. Oh lord, save me now. My ovaries were putting out the welcoming rug for the man. Nope, no, not happening, I reminded them.

"Is that everyone?" Rebecca asked as she floated down the stairs wrapped in pale blue silk. She was epitome of classy and refined. I glanced down at myself. I managed pretty, and at a push mysterious if I went heavy on the eyeliner. The simple little black dress I'd been forced into wrapped up my breasts and gave me a cleavage Miss Parton would be proud of. The skirt was floaty and skimmed my thighs. Rebecca had strapped skyscrapers on my feet that made me long for my sneakers and pj shorts. Four hours and counting I promised them.

"We are just waiting for Jazzy and April."

Rebecca nodded. "Ah yes, from the group."

"What group?" I didn't get to go to any group.

"Jazzy and April are coming?" Sebastian asked. "From the group?"

"What group!"

Sebastian raised his hands. "Hey, if you know, you know. You know?"

I leveled him with my Roberts stare and folded my arms. "Clearly not."

A round of giggling echoed from down my drive, and three figures emerged from the darkness.

"Lucifer?" I asked, staring at the pretty girls he had attached to each arm. "It's meant to be a singles night, where you pick up the women at the event, not before."

He smirked as he got closer, ever comfortable in his three piece suit, complete with pocket watch today. "I found these two lovely ladies staggering along the road on their way here. I thought with all the things that go bump in the night around your property, I'd be the perfect gentleman and escort them here safely."

Natia's head popped out over my shoulder and she snorted. "Perfect gentleman."

He cocked a brow at her as he ushered the two women up my steps. "Jazzy and April?" I checked.

"I'm April," the girl on the left said.

The other one - Jazzy - jumped up and down for a whole minute, wow that girl has energy. I was worn out just looking at her. "Omg, we are here - in White Castle with Cora."

"And Hudson, don't forget him," April said. Something hot flared in my chest. Indigestion. I needed stronger antacids.

Natia eyeballed them both. "Is that Natia Waterford?" Jazzy asked. "Oh. My. God. Is Archan here?" She glanced down at her boobs and made sure they were on maximum display whilst still maintaining a PG rating.

"He is," Natia said leaning against the doorframe. She was calm, too calm. Oh boy.

April blinked like she'd just realized who they'd been verbally fucking Archan in front of.

"Don't worry we're married," April said.

"Oh," I exclaimed. "Why are you at a singles night?"

Jazzy shrugged. "Always room for a book boyfriend."

I frowned at her, what were the odds? Maybe this group they secretly went to was for the crazy women who believed the rest of us were fictional characters? Clearly Jennifer-Lynn also attended the group.

I waved the rest of them in and let Sebastian and Maggie settle them into their correct spots.

"Hey, Cora," Rebecca said, flicking through the list on my clipboard. I was organized, in fact I was the organizer which meant I didn't need to participate, I'd be too busy overseeing everything and maintaining order.

"Yes?"

"We are short one girl."

What? No, I'd specifically made sure that wouldn't happen, that's why I was the organizer. I'd organized myself out of the equation. "Let me see," I huffed, grabbing the clipboard.

"Lucifer!" I barked. He winked at me from his position against the makeshift bar in the dining room. Lucifer wasn't meant to be here. But I wasn't about to shove the devil out of the door. I might need a favor from him in the future.

"It will be okay," Rebecca said, prying the clipboard from my hands and guiding me towards an empty seat behind a little table. I was between Jennifer-Lynn and Jazzy. This felt like a set up. I spied Hudson eyeballing my every move with a predator's gleam. Ugh.

Maggie stepped into the center of the parlor and clapped her hands, gaining everyone's attention. She blushed, then cleared her throat. "You got this," I mouthed.

The boys made their way over, some I knew, others I didn't. All were supernatural.

Hudson zeroed in on me and strides over with purpose. He elbow checked a younger vampire named Fred out of the way before folding himself into the empty chair opposite mine. I guess if I get this out of the way, I could relax, maybe even enjoy myself.

I picked up the sheet of questions in front of me and groaned. The bell signaled the start. "What's the weirdest thing you've ever dreamed?" I asked.

Hudson's eyes lit up with amusement. Jennifer-Lynn asked the same question of Zee.

"Well, beautiful, I'm a little bit of a freak in the bedroom," Zee started.

"Not just the bedroom," Natia muttered as she placed a glass of wine in front of Jennifer.

"Also not what she asked," I added.

"Worst joke?" Zee said getting back on script.

"Did it hurt?" Jennifer-Lynn asked.

"What when I fell from heaven?"

They both cracked up.

"Two minutes," Hudson said.

"What?"

"Two minutes of your undivided attention, that's what this calls for."

I blinked. He was right, where were my manners? That's right, hanging out with my ovaries that had packed their bags and ran off in protest.

"Well, what's the weirdest thing you've ever dreamed?" I asked again.

He leaned forward and unconsciously I copied him, like it was some big secret. Who knows, maybe it is? "The weirdest thing I dreamed, was that you stopped fighting this thing between us. That you gave into your desires and stopped living in fear. The weirdest thing I dreamed was that you let me kiss, lick, and bite every inch-" my eyes dropped to his lips.

"Next question!" I shouted as I leaned back and far far away from him.

He glanced down. "Who would you want to be stuck on an island with?"

"Nobody, people talk too much."

"Girl! Same!" Jazzy squealed next to me and held her hand up. I high fived her and smiled. Maybe I should go to this group, these women seemed pretty cool. Who cared if they were crazy living in a fantasy world? We all needed to escape from time to time.

Harry floated around the room, offering advice to the patrons who couldn't hear him. Good job really, or Hudson would have just been told to 'stop acting like an overgrown house cat, have some decorum, and treat a lady as she's meant to be treated.' Whatever that meant.

"What one word would friends use to describe you?" I asked. *Arrogant.*

He tilted his head to the side. "Perceptive."

Natia whooped from across the room and hugged April. "I found my sarcasm buddy," she shouted.

Well, if we didn't manage any romantic matches, we were certainly matching friends.

"Time's up," Maggie declared with a little tap on the bell.

Hudson folded his arms and glared at me. I raised a brow at him. Two minutes, over and done, Principal, move it along.

"Dude, rotate," Zee said.

Hudson glanced at him. "Not you."

Zee rolled his eyes. "Fine, I'll skip your lady, and move on to the beautiful Jazzy."

"Dave," Hudson growled. Dangerous Dave materialized behind Hudson like fog. How did he do that? "Take my chair."

"It's not your chair," I muttered as Hudson stood and swapped places with Dave.

Hudson paused with his hand on the back of the chair. "Do you want me to leave?"

"Yes."

"Then stop antagonizing my animal, Cora."

I blinked as Dave replaced him and Hudson paused in front of Rebecca's chair before folding himself into it.

"He's been considerate of your feelings," Dave said.

My eyes snapped to him. "What feelings?"

Dave sighed. "Are you seriously this emotionally stilted? Teenagers have a better clue what's going on around them than you."

"What about you, Dave? Any ladies catch your eye tonight?"

"No, not tonight. I'm here to make sure you two make it to the other side of the evening without killing each other."

"Now those are more accurate feelings."

"It's a fine line you know."

"What is?"

"Between love and hate."

"Save me the waxing poetic, Dave. You've never minced your words before now."

"He's right though," Jennifer-Lynn leaned in ignoring her partner's monologue on why he'd like to have dinner with Edward Cullen. "You and Hudson need to get your head out of your asses and just get on with it already."

Jazzy waved a hand in her partner's face, cutting him off, and leaned in on my other side. "We waited a whole book for this, you can't keep us hanging on forever. There's slow burn, then there's asleep."

"A book?" I asked just as April abandoned her seat altogether and came to stand behind Dave.

Dave eyeballed the women like he was assessing their threat level. "Yes, book one, where you two meet and eye fuck each other for chapters," April said with a nod. "Enough already, bump uglies or I'll take him."

Another bout of heartburn. Damn that was brutal, I should lay off the cookies. "I'm not clueless, nor am I eye fucking Hudson. No fucking is happening ladies - if you're hard up watch some porn. Or take Zee home."

"The book is always better," Jennifer-Lynn stated wistfully.

"Agreed, unless you are *in* the book," Jazzy said with a long gaze at Lucifer. "Then it's time to live out those book boyfriend fantasies."

Lucifer winked at her, Jazzy almost did a full on swoon. Dave even shifted, ever ready to catch the damsel.

"Time's up," Maggie declared and rang the bell.

Hudson shot out of his chair and swapped with Dave seamlessly. I folded my arms and arched a brow.

The girls ignored their new partners and eyeballed the pair of us like we were their new favorite TV show. "Are you a boomerang?" I asked.

"No," he drawled.

"Then why do you keep coming back?"

"Oooo burn," April whispered.

Hudson ignored my new friends and leaned across the table. He snapped his hand out, wrapped it around the back of my neck and planted his lips on mine. Oh. My. God. I melted. Instant puddle on the chair. His lips were hot and insistent on mine, sending ripples of pleasure down my spine. His tongue began to dance with mine.

"Hey, free show. Where's the popcorn?" Zee shouted.

"Dude, I'd stay clear of him if I were you." Zac advised. Yes, go away. Everyone go away. "Shifters are notoriously jealous and territorial. Partially those at the beginning of the mating heat."

The what? My mind screeched to a halt and I pulled back from Hudson. He let me go. A self satisfied grin on his lips. "I'll always come back, Cora, the faster you learn that the sooner we can get on with our lives - together."

He stood and nodded at Dave, they both exited the house with a cocky stride. The door clicked closed behind them.

"Close your mouth," Rebecca muttered to me as she left her guy.

"But he's so arrogant."

"He's also gorgeous," Jennifer-Lynn stated with a dreamy look.

"And alpha, so alpha," April added.

"Also hot damn, that voice," Jazzy added.

"So what are you waiting for, girl?" Jennifer-Lynn asked.

I blinked at the closed door. What was I waiting for…?

I smiled. Let the games begin.

Diary of the White Furry Menace

This woman smells funny, not of death like the disgusting male I rode in on, but not of life either. She's a conundrum, I should stay and ensure she doesn't pose a threat.

She attempted to sell me immediately, I am not a feline to be manhandled. I explain this to her and she relented immediately. She's a pushover.

I watch carefully as Cora discusses the dead with the vampire. He's attractive as far as vampires go, he's stealthy and slinks across the floor in a way a feline can appreciate. He throws knives at her, which she dodges, they don't seem to be arguing though, maybe it's a strange courtship ritual I'm not aware of? Either way she's missing the point of the way to a man's heart, it's not through his brain or brawn, it's through his stomach. I shall demonstrate.

She named me the white furry menace, so when danger arrives at the door, I ensure the intruder knows he will face my wrath should he try to enter. The pretty blonde vampire, and the dumb elemental sit on the floor whilst I demonstrate my superiority. The evil that lurks speeds off at the sight of me. There, now perhaps she'll feed me freshly cooked chicken, the odd salmon too. After all, without me they'd be lost. How did they survive this long without me?

The wolf is clearly displeased with Cora, again she misses the fact that all males regardless of species, even smelly dogs, can be soothed with food. I shall demonstrate.

It's Cora's birthday, and she's served the one clearly after her attentions, fruit. His beast ripples below the surface, like mine. Again, I will demonstrate the need to satisfy a male through his stomach. She glared at my offering, again. Apparently, you can't teach stupid.

Printed in Great Britain
by Amazon